THIS CANDLEWICK BOOK BELONGS TO:

_____

_____

_____

_____

To Lucienne
L. H.

Text copyright © 1995 by Martin Waddell
Illustrations copyright © 1995 by Leo Hartas

Second U.S. edition 1998

Library of Congress Catalog Card Number 95-71370

ISBN 0-7636-0588-3

2 4 6 8 10 9 7 5 3 1

Printed in Hong Kong

This book was typeset in Garamond.
The pictures were done in pen and ink and watercolor.

Candlewick Press
2067 Massachusetts Avenue
Cambridge, Massachusetts 02140

Mimi
and the
Picnic

MARTIN WADDELL
illustrated by
LEO HARTAS

CANDLEWICK PRESS
CAMBRIDGE, MASSACHUSETTS

Mimi lived with her mouse sisters
and brothers beneath the big tree.
The mice came in all sizes, but the
smallest of all was called Hugo.

One day they all went for a picnic
on the bank of the river.

Mimi laid out a lovely lunch for her
sisters and brothers.

Hugo sat on his Big Leaf and
watched her, while the sisters
and brothers ran off to play.

They played . . .   and they played . . .

and they played . . .

and they played . . .

and they played . . .   and they played.

But when they came back for their lunch, Hugo's Big Leaf was empty. There was no sign of Hugo at all!

"Hugo's so small he'd be easily lost," Mimi said. "We'd better start looking for Hugo right away!"

The mouse sisters and brothers scurried about, under the leaves, and around Robin's Nest, and up Badger's Path by the two Rusty Tins, and down by Mole's Hole.

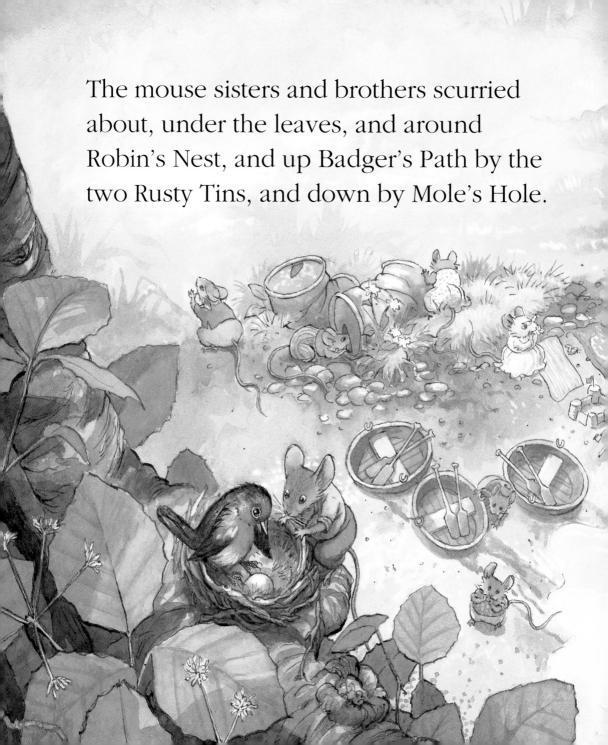

"Hugo's so small we can't find him at all,"
the mouse sisters and brothers told Mimi.
"Try looking some more!" Mimi said.

And they looked . . .   and they looked . . .

and they looked . . .

and they looked . . .

and they looked.

And then they looked a lot more – some of them looked where they'd looked before! "Hugo's lost," Mimi said.

The sisters and brothers and Mimi were very upset. Hugo was *so* small, and all of them loved him a lot.

Mimi sat down on Hugo's Big Leaf and started to cry.
Great big mouse tears rolled down her cheeks, and her mouse sisters and brothers cried too, for they all loved little Hugo so much.

They cried . . .

and they cried . . .

and they cried . . .

and they cried . . .

and they cried.

AND THEN . . .

They found Hugo, but he
wasn't as small as he was before . . .

for he'd had a *very* big lunch!

MARTIN WADDELL is one of the most prolific and successful children's writers of his time, having written more than a hundred books for children, including *Can't You Sleep, Little Bear?*; *Let's Go Home, Little Bear*; *You and Me, Little Bear*; *Farmer Duck*; *Owl Babies*; and *When the Teddy Bears Came*. He has won numerous awards for his work, which *The Horn Book* has deemed "deliciously sly" and *School Library Journal* has called "outrageously funny."

LEO HARTAS has illustrated numerous books for children, including two other books about Mimi and her mouse family, *Mimi's Christmas* and *Mimi and the Dream House*.